Emma Kate

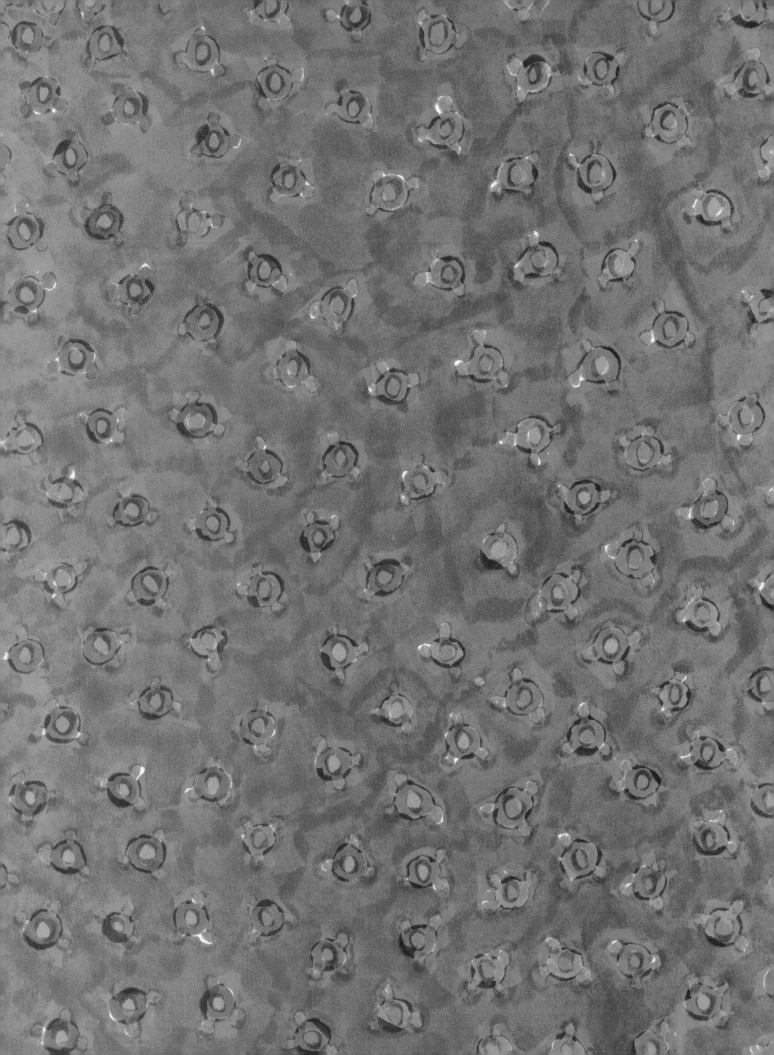

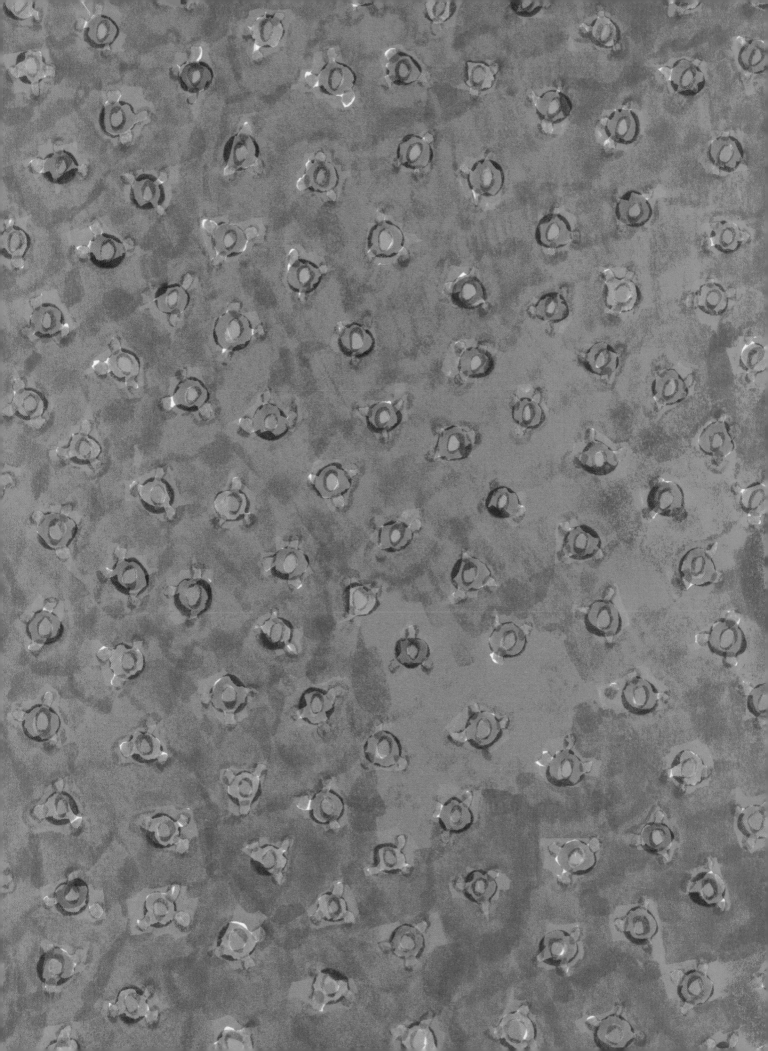

Emma Kate

To Dr. Seuss and Horton

PATRICIA LEE GAUCH, EDITOR

No part of this publication may be reproduced, stored in a retrieval system, or
transmitted in any form or by any means, electronic, mechanical, photocopying,
recording, or otherwise, without written permission of the publisher. For
information regarding permission, write to Philomel Books, a member of
Penguin Young Readers Group, a division of Penguin Group (USA) Inc.,
345 Hudson Street, New York, NY 10014.

ISBN-13: 978-0-545-00001-7
ISBN-10: 0-545-00001-7

12 11 10 9 8 7 6 5 4 3 2 1   7 8 9 10 11 12/0

Printed in the U.S.A.   40

This edition first printing, January 2007

Design by Semadar Megged

The text was set in Optima.

The art was done in pencils and markers.

Emma Kate

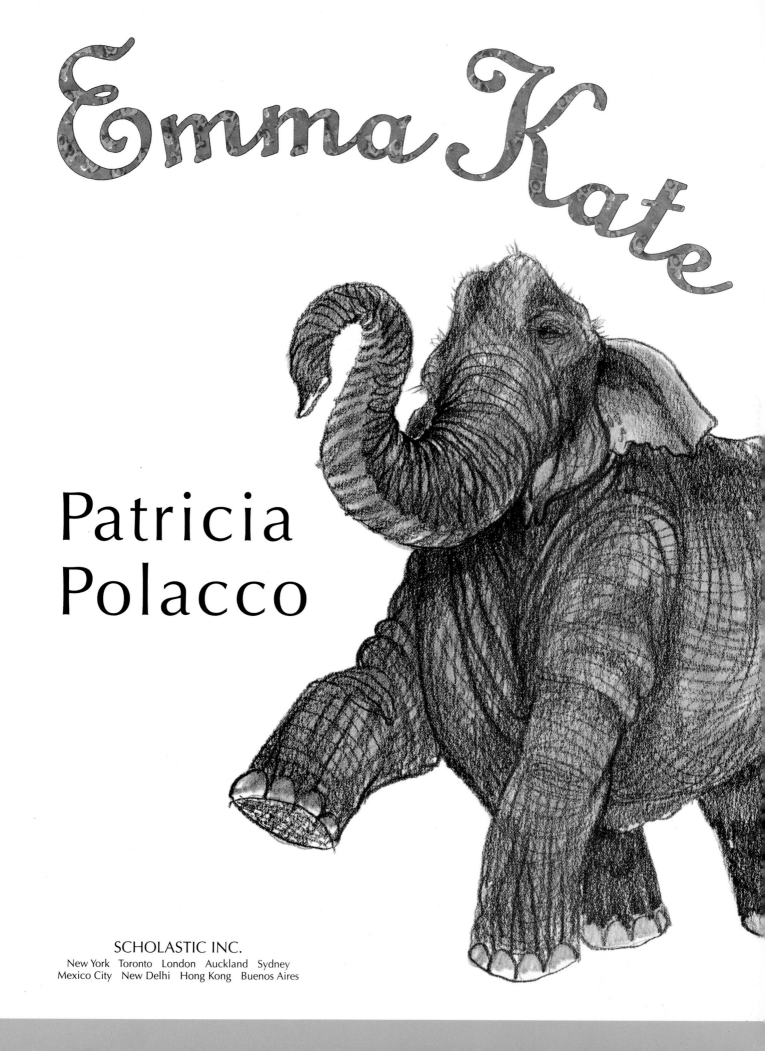

Patricia Polacco

SCHOLASTIC INC.

New York Toronto London Auckland Sydney
Mexico City New Delhi Hong Kong Buenos Aires

Emma Kate is my best friend.

We do just about everything together!

We walk to school together every morning.

She sits next to me in class.

We play together at recess.

We sit together in the café-gym-a-torium at lunch.

When we get home from school,
we ride our bikes together.

We do our homework together, too!
Sometimes, even on a school night, she stays over.

She loves my pet mouse Gwendolyn.

On weekends, Momma drives us to soccer practice.

We take long walks and watch the clouds in the sky.
Most of all we love to read together.

One day Emma Kate got a real sore throat . . .
—and so did I!
When we went to see the doctor, the doctor said that we would have to have our tonsils out.

So we went to the hospital and got our tonsils out . . .
—then we both ate gallons of pink ice cream!

Emma Kate is my best friend.

We take our baths together.
Then we climb into bed.

Sometimes, when nighttime comes and I'm in my bed, I tell Momma and Daddy all about Emma Kate and the things we do together.

They just smile and say, "You and your Emma Kate. You have such an imagination. Good night, sweetpea. Sweet dreams."

Then they both give me a big kiss and tuck me in.

And I dream of Emma Kate.

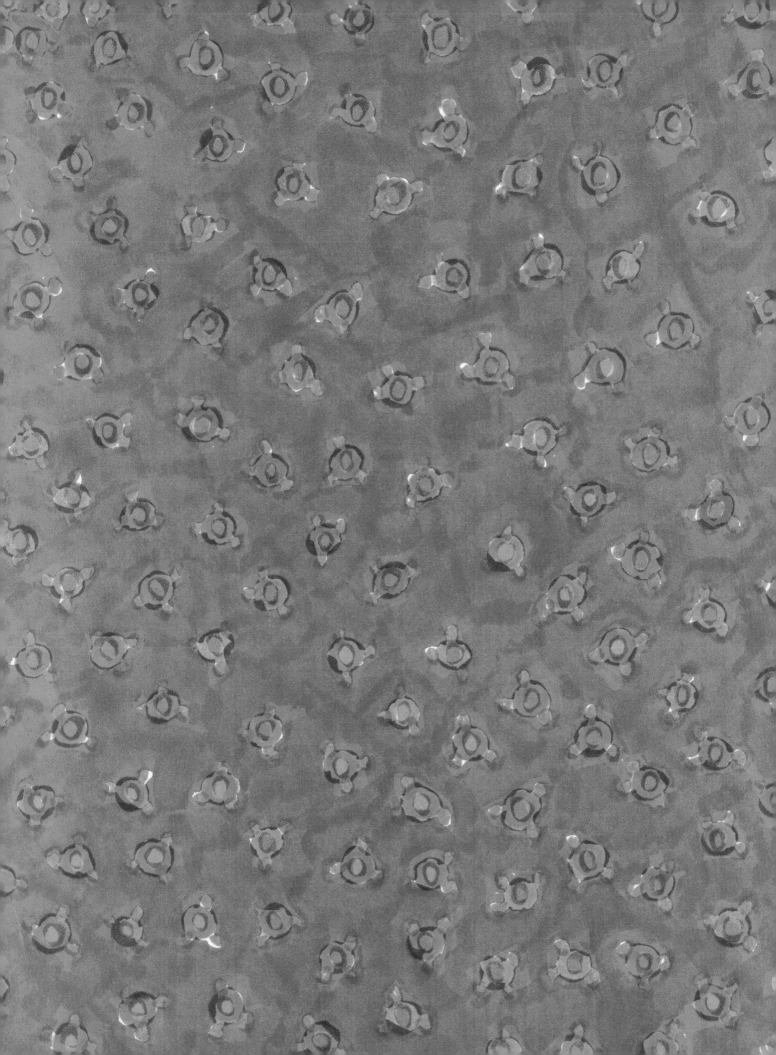

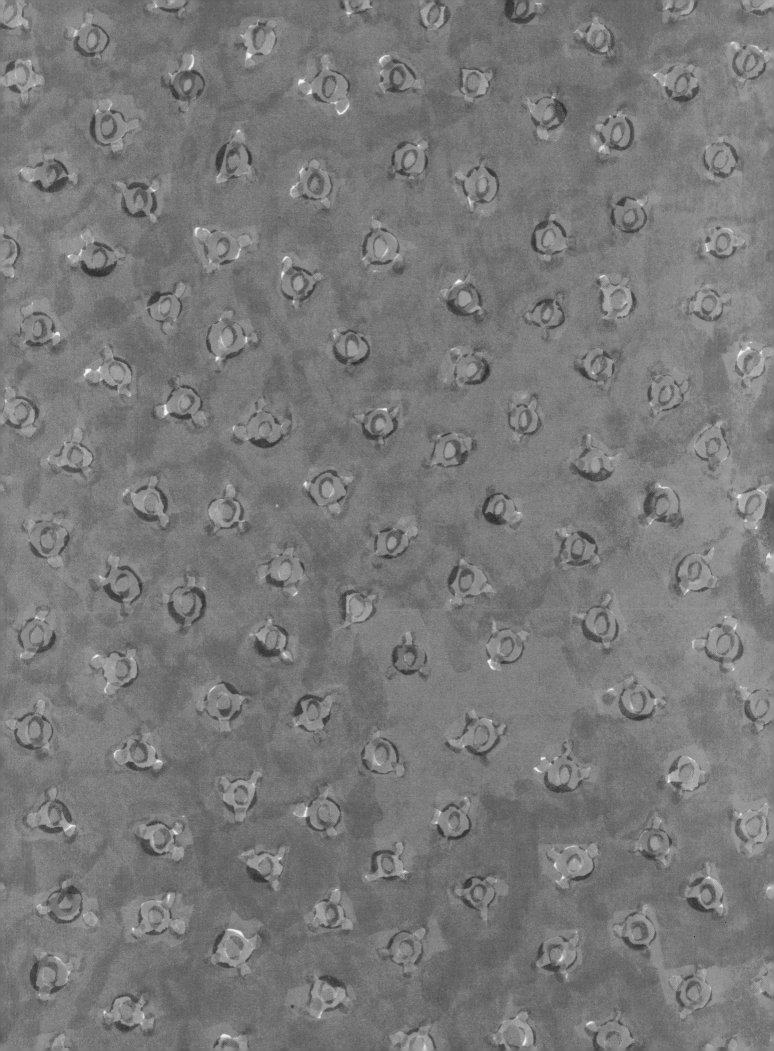